This baby lion is ready to go.
He wants to find his friends and say hello.

Baby giraffe looks hungry to me,
Licking the leaves that grow on the tree.

Say Hello
to the
Baby Animals!

Ian Whybrow Ed Eaves

Say Hello
to the
Baby Animals!

MACMILLAN CHILDREN'S BOOKS

Baby hippopotamus loves to keep cool.
What a lot of noise when he jumps in the pool!

Hello, baby monkey!

Oo, oo, oo!

I can see a funny face. Can you see it, too?
It's a baby monkey and he's waving at you!

Hello, baby giraffe!

Lick, lick, lick!

Hello, baby hippo!

Splish, splash, splosh!

These little zebras love to run around.
Their hooves click-clack on the hard dry ground.

Hello, baby zebras!

Click-clack, click-clack!

Who's this going squawk, squawk, squawk?
It's a baby parrot and he loves to talk.

This baby elephant is having fun,
Squirting mud at everyone.

Hello, baby elephant!

Squirt, squirt, squirt!

Here's a baby leopard, walking down the track.
Give him a roar and he'll roar back!

Hello, baby leopard!

Raaaaaaaaaah!

What a lot of babies, my, oh my!
It must be time to say goodbye.

Goodbye, baby monkey!
OO, OO, OO!

Goodbye, baby giraffe!
Lick, lick, lick!

Goodbye, baby elephant!
Squirt, squirt, squirt!

Goodbye, baby hippo!
Splish, splash, splosh!

Goodbye, baby parrot!
Squawk, Squawk, Squawk!

Goodbye, baby zebras!
Click-clack, click-clack!

Goodbye, baby leopard!
Raaaaaaaaaaah!

Look at baby lion, cuddled up tight.
Purr very quietly and say night-night.

For Ella Rose
and Teddy – I.W.

For Mum – E.E.

First published 2006 by Macmillan Children's Books
This edition published 2007 by Macmillan Children's Books
a division of Macmillan Publishers Limited
20 New Wharf Road, London N1 9RR
Basingstoke and Oxford
Associated companies throughout the world
www.panmacmillan.com

ISBN: 978-1-4050-9024-7

Text copyright © Ian Whybrow 2006
Illustrations copyright © Edward Eaves 2006
Moral rights asserted.

9

A CIP catalogue record for this book is available from the British Library.

Printed in China